espresso
education

Phonics

The Magic Dragon

Gill Budgell

W
FRANKLIN WATTS
LONDON • SYDNEY

First published in 2012 by
Franklin Watts
338 Euston Road
London NW1 3BH

Franklin Watts Australia
Level 17/207 Kent Street
Sydney NSW 2000

Text and illustration © Franklin Watts 2012

The Espresso characters are originated and
designed by Claire Underwood and Pesky Ltd.

The Espresso characters are the property of
Espresso Education Ltd.

A CIP catalogue record for this book is
available from the British Library.

ISBN: 978 1 4451 0755 4 (hbk)
ISBN: 978 1 4451 0758 5 (pbk)

Illustrations by Artful Doodlers Ltd.
Art Director: Jonathan Hair
Series Editor: Jackie Hamley
Project Manager: Gill Budgell
Series Designer: Matthew Lilly

Printed in China

Franklin Watts is a division of
Hachette Children's Books,
an Hachette UK company.

www.hachette.co.uk

Level 1 50 words
Concentrating on CVC words plus and, the, to

Level 2 70 words
Concentrating on double letter sounds and new letter
sounds (ck, ff, ll, ss, j, v, w, x, y, z, zz) plus no, go, I

Level 3 100 words
Concentrating on new graphemes (qu, ch, sh, th, ng,
ai, ee, igh, oa, oo, ar, or, ur, ow, oi, ear, air, ure, er)
plus he, she, we, me, be, was, my, you, they, her, all

Level 4 150 words
Concentrating on adjacent consonants (CVCC/CCVC
words) plus said, so, have, like, some, come, were, there,
little, one, do, when, out, what

Level 5 180 words
Concentrating on new graphemes (ay, wh, ue, ir, ou, aw,
ph, ew, ea, a-e, e-e, i-e, o-e, u-e) plus day, very, put, time,
about, saw, here, came, made, don't, asked, looked,
called, Mrs

Level 6 200 words
Concentrating on alternative pronunciations (c, ow, o, g, y)
and spellings (ee, ur, ay, or, m, n, air, l, r) plus your, don't
time, saw, here, very, make, their, called, asked, looked

Sal took Eddy to see a show called 'The Magic Dragon'.

"Are dragons scary?" asked Eddy.
"No, not the dragon in this show,"
said Sal.
So Eddy was happy.

The
Magic
Dragon

They sat down and
the show began.

The dragon was huge.
He was gentle.
He was magic …

"Do you fancy a trip?" asked
the dragon.
"Can I go, Sal?" asked Eddy.
"Yes, but hold on with both hands.
And don't be too long!"
said Sal.

9

"Where shall we go?"
the dragon asked.
"Can we fly to Egypt to see
a pyramid?" said Eddy.

10

"Off we go! High in the sky!" said the dragon.

They flew for a long time.
Eddy looked down and
saw a pyramid.

"Wow!" he yelled.
"It's very hot here."
"I can make you cool,"
said the dragon.

13

So they flew again.
Eddy looked down and saw
snow and ice below.
"Wow!" he yelled. "It's very,
very cold here!"

"Don't worry. You are in no danger," said the dragon. "I am a magic dragon. I can keep you warm."

"And I can carry you back
to Sal now," he said.
And he did.

"Did you enjoy the show?"
asked Sal.
"Oh yes. It was magic!"
Eddy said.

Puzzle Time

Same letters, different sounds.

Find the six pairs.

One has been done for you.

Look out! They will be the same letters but you will have to say them differently.

no

long

dragon

bold

yes

snow

on

ice

down

cat

danger

fly

long – bold is already completed to show the first pair.
In **long** the **o** is pronounced as **/o/** whilst in **bold** the **o** is pronounced more like **/oa/**.

o – no, on   **ow** – snow, down   **y** – fly, yes
c – ice, cat   **g** – danger, dragon

A note about the phonics in this book

Alternative pronunciations of known phonemes

Known grapheme and phoneme	New ways to say grapheme	Words in the story
c as /k/	/k/	can, cool, cold
	/s/	fancy, ice
ow as /ow/	/ow/	down, now, wow
	/oa/	show, snow, below
o as /o/	/o/	not, long
	/oa/	go, so, no, don't, both
g as /g/	/g/	dragon, go
	/j/	magic, huge, gentle, Egypt, danger
y as /y/	/y/	yes, yelled
	/igh/	fly, sky
	/i/	Egypt, pyramid
	/ee/	scary, happy, very, worry, carry
common words	time, saw, here, very, make	
tricky common words	called, asked, looked	

Remind children about the letters they already know for these phonemes.

In the puzzle they are challenged to match the words that have the same sound in them; the same letters but different pronunciation. Pronunciation always depends on where you live so say them the way you normally do!

Top tip: if a child gets stuck on a word then ask them to try and sound it out and then blend it together again or show them how to do this. For example, dragon, d-r-a-g-o-n, dragon.